MW01488879

INTRODUCTION

As a child, I thought I had special parents because all of my friends wanted to be adopted by them. Now as an adult, I know my parents are extraordinarily special because all of my adult friends want to be adopted. To come home from school each day to a home filled with the essence of fresh baked cookies or Daddy serenading Mom, gave each of us children a feeling of love and contentment that words can not describe. I have learned so much more about the struggles they had as we grew up. From tuberculosis to cancer they were tested for 15 years. Rarely did we children feel the strain, stress or worry that was upon our family. The gift for parenting that Daddy and Mom have to this day is one in a million and my brothers and I often say, "How blessed we were to have chosen by God to have been born to Richard and Carmelita Silanskas." I have a 'passion' for motherhood that I gleaned from watching my mother. Sure, the daily chores do seem to add up and the mounds of laundry seem never to diminish, but as I learned from my Hero and Mentor, I would have it no other way. Actually, I can honestly say, what will I do when the laundry does go away…to college?

Please, Dear Lord, Make the Laundry Go Away

© 2005 Elm Hill Books
ISBN: 1-404-18553-4
Printed in Mexico

The quoted ideas expressed in this book (but not scripture verses) are not, in all cases, exact quotations, as some have been edited for clarity and brevity. In all cases, the author has attempted to maintain the speaker's original intent. In some cases, quoted material for this book was obtained from secondary sources, primarily print media. While every effort was made to ensure the accuracy of these sources, the accuracy cannot be guaranteed. For additions, deletions, corrections or clarifications in future editions of this text, please write Elm Hill Books or e-mail pshepherd@elmhillbooks.com

Products from Elm Hill Books may be purchased in bulk for educational, business, fundraising, or sales promotional use. For information, please email SpecialMarkets@ThomasNelson.com

PLEASE, DEAR LORD, MAKE THE LAUNDRY GO AWAY

The Beginning...

...for richer
or poorer,
in sickness and
in health,
to love and honor,
'till death
we do part.

As a Bride,
my concerns
were all
about him,

preparing his
favorite foods
and trying
to stay slim.

Each day an
anniversary,
we ne're seemed
to miss,

from the day
we first met,
to the time
we first kissed.

Our life
was complete
with God and
each other,

or this,
so I thought,
'till I became
a Mother.

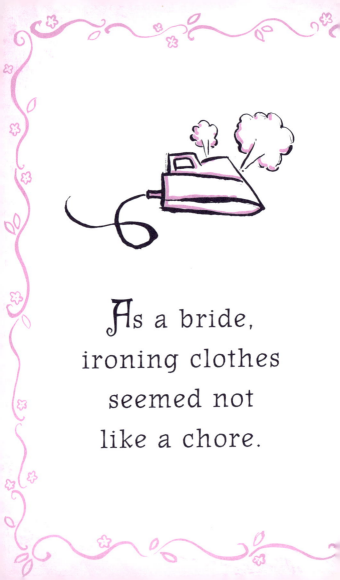

As a bride,
ironing clothes
seemed not
like a chore.

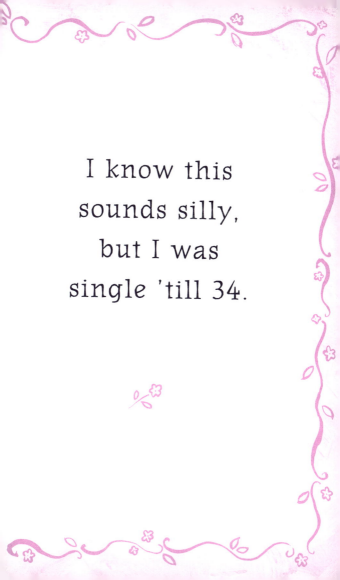

I know this
sounds silly,
but I was
single 'till 34.

But now
as a Mom, I can
honestly say,

Please, dear Lord,
make this laundry
go away!

As a bride,
I would rush,
before he'd
wake up,

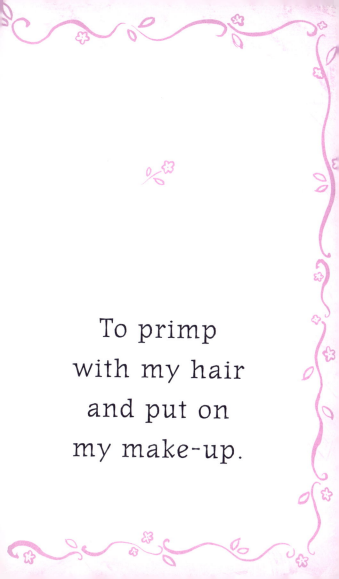

To primp
with my hair
and put on
my make-up.

Now, as a Mom,
my day starts
with a song,
the lyrics, the
same...a cry
that's sooo long.

Without placing
my feet upon
the floor,
I fly through
the room and
out of the door.

There lies my
tiny angel, so
helpless and sad,
Hungry and wet
is what makes
her feel bad.

I love that she knows me, her Mommy is here, Just one simple touch seems to dry up her tear.

The tasks
of each day
are many,
that's true,

for now, we've
been blessed
with a family...
that's two.

From morning
'till night, we play,
feed and diaper,
I laugh to myself,
thinking Dad
wanted a Viper.

Now, it's the
mini-van we drive
out in style,
as couples go past
in convertibles
and smile!

As a bride,
I could grab
my purse and
run out,
I'd shop and
have lunch;
YOU KNOW,
"a girl's day out."

To run to the
store is no longer
a joy, with a
two-year-old girl
and a tiny new boy.

I've invented a
dance called The
Mommy Square,
I know all new
Moms have surely
been there.

You step to the right and prep the diaper bag, with a step to the left, some toys you do grab.

Place a child on a hip and turn around slow, then pick up the second and away you go!

As a bride,
off to work with
a kiss and a smile,
looking forward
to see him in just
a short while.

I'd count down
the hours 'till we'd
be together,
having dinner and
cuddling like two
birds of a feather.

Now 24/7,
I'm blessed,
staying at home,
the words come
out clearly
in this old
simple poem...

"A Father's
work is from
sun to sun, But a
Mother's work
Is NEVER done."

Sure, I love tiny
fingers, reaching
under the door,
as they peek in the
bathroom, while
lying on the floor.

"Mooomy, what'cha doin'?" They sing in harmony, "I'll be out in one moment," so they wait patiently.

Why do they love
to stay close,
under foot?
Entertained, as
they watch me
launder and cook?

I fall asleep each night with a tear in my eye, for I know we've been blessed and not a day will go by,

Without thanks to the Lord, for "I am a Mother," this fills me with joy, unlike any other.

Each morning,
I await, their
faces to see,

when they rise
from their beds
and rush to me.

Sure I have
my days
when I'm tired
and feel blue,

but I'll
never resent
my cute
little two.

"Don't you need YOUR time?" Many have asked.

I can't
say I do, for
these moments
soon pass.

I've known in my
heart they will
quickly "outgrow
me," so, from one
Mom to the next, I
offer this plea...

Please see your child
as a gift from above,
and cherish each
moment they fill you
with love.

They look in your
eyes with trust and
with faith, for you
are a hero, that
none can replace.

The cooking,
the LAUNDRY, do
seem to add up,
but don't let these
things make
you miss them
GROW UP.

A Prayer and a
butterfly kiss at
night's end,
I look forward
'till morning, when
it all starts again!

BĬO

Dianne Garvis is a singer, songwriter and powerful motivational speaker. She has been featured in such magazines as *Charisma* and *New Covenant* and has been a guest of the 700 club. As founder/director of 'The Good Neighbor Program, inc.' in Florida, Dianne is using her gifts to bring hope to those who have lost hope by teaming together communities to reach out and make a difference, 'one person at a time.'

After 12 years of serious medical problems, Dianne had nearly lost hope of one day having a family. It was her faith that kept her going, and now she and her husband John have two 'miracle' children. Her passion for motherhood is evident in every area of her life. Everywhere she goes, people fall in love with her singing, moving testimony and humble spirit on stage and off. It is seldom that you will meet such a total package of commitment, talent and yielded spirit to Christ as Dianne.